Treasure's Day at Sea

By Andrea Posner-Sanchez
Illustrated by Sue DiCicco

A GOLDEN BOOK • NEW YORK

Copyright © 2015 Disney Enterprises, Inc. All rights reserved. Published in the United States by Golden Books, an imprint of Random House Children's Books, a division of Random House LLC, 1745 Broadway, New York, NY 10019, and in Canada by Random House of Canada Limited, Toronto, Penguin Random House Companies, in conjunction with Disney Enterprises, Inc. Golden Books, A Golden Book, A Little Golden Book, the G colophon, and the distinctive gold spine are registered trademarks of Random House LLC.
randomhousekids.com
ISBN 978-0-7364-3335-8 (trade) — 978-0-7364-3336-5 (ebook)
Printed in the United States of America
10 9 8 7 6 5 4 3

One sunny day, Ariel's pet kitten, Treasure, was
playing on the beach with her friends. Treasure and
Max the dog were running along the shore, happily
getting their paws wet. Scuttle the seagull flew nearby,
telling funny stories.

All of a sudden, the friends heard a *tap-tap-tap*.
"Was that you, Scuttle?" Treasure asked.
Scuttle shook his head. "I *auk-auk-auk* and even
caw-caw-caw sometimes, but I never *tap-tap-tap*," the
seagull replied.

The *tap-tap-tap* sound continued. Max scampered up a sand dune and looked around. He pointed a paw out toward the ocean. That was where the sound was coming from.

Treasure, being a very curious kitten, wanted to investigate. She leaped onto a piece of driftwood and floated out into the water.

Treasure soon passed a dolphin doing some
amazing leaps. But the dolphin wasn't making any
tapping sounds.

Then Treasure floated by a pair of sunbathing
seals. They waved their flippers but didn't make any
*tap-tap-tap*s.

"I see something!" Scuttle reported from overhead.
"Turn a bit more to the left."

Treasure used her paws to paddle her driftwood
boat. The *tap-tap-tap*s were getting louder!

Soon the kitten spotted a sea otter! Treasure
watched as the otter lifted a clamshell and banged it
on a rock she balanced on her belly. *Tap-tap-tap.*

"Hi, I'm Treasure. What are you doing?"
the kitten asked.

"I'm Pearl. I'm eating my lunch," the sea otter explained. After a few more *tap-tap-tap*s, the shell cracked open and Pearl slurped out the yummy clam. Treasure was impressed!

"It must be fun to eat at sea," Treasure said. "I eat all my meals on land."

"Sea otters do most everything in the water," Pearl told her. "We eat, play, and even sleep here!"

That sounded like a great way to live—especially to a kitten who loved the sea! Treasure called up to Scuttle, "I'm going to spend the day in the water with Pearl. I'll tell you and Max all about it later."

"I'm a bit hungry," Treasure told Pearl after Scuttle flew away. "Do you think you can help me get some food?"

"Sure," said Pearl. "I'll dive down and see what I can find."

Treasure treaded water while Pearl swam all the way down to the sea floor. Even though sea otters live in shallow waters, it was too deep for a kitten.

Pearl soon swam back up with a sea urchin for each of them. The sea urchins were purple and spiky and didn't look anything like the food Princess Ariel fed to Treasure!

"Actually, I'm not that hungry anymore," Treasure
fibbed. "You can eat mine, too."

Pearl banged the urchin on a rock until its shell
broke. She happily ate the soft insides.

"After eating, I usually groom myself to keep nice and clean," said Pearl. "You want to see?" The sweet otter rubbed her fur while twisting and turning and even doing somersaults.

Treasure gave it a try. But before long, the poor
kitten was miserable. Her nose and ears were filled
with water.

"Sorry about that," said Pearl. "I didn't know
your nostrils and ears don't close up in the water like
mine do."

Treasure was exhausted. She might not have been able to swim as well as a sea otter, or eat the same food, but she was sure she could nap just as well!

Treasure flipped onto her back and closed her eyes, like Pearl did. Now, this was relaxing!

"Treasure! Treasure!" yelled Pearl. "Wake up!"

The kitten woke with a start and was surprised to find herself on the opposite side of the cove.

"What happened?" Treasure yelled back.

"I forgot to tell you to wrap some kelp around yourself so you don't float away," Pearl explained.

"I think it's time for me to head home," Treasure told Pearl. "I'll always love the sea, but being on land is pretty great, too."

"Maybe I'll come visit you someday," said the sea otter.

Back on shore, Max and Scuttle were thrilled to see Treasure.

"Hiya, kid," called Scuttle. "How was your day?"

"I learned that living in the sea is great—if you're a sea otter," said Treasure. "I'll stick to playing in the water, but I'll eat and sleep on land!"

Then Treasure gave presents to her friends. Scuttle
got a lovely kelp scarf. Max got some rocks that were
perfect for cracking clamshells—or just playing fetch.

"Now let's head home!" Treasure called, running
toward Princess Ariel's palace. "I'm starving!"